A SPECTACULAR STORY
FROM THE FUTURE

I dedicate this book to my grandmother, Nora Lally.
Thank you for the old stories, card games,
and your wonderfully delicious brown cake.

A SPECTACULAR STORY FROM THE FUTURE

First Wonderland Works edition • November 2021

ISBN: 978-1-7399268-0-9

WONDERLAND WORKS
County Mayo • Ireland

A SPECTACULAR STORY FROM THE FUTURE

WRITTEN AND ILLUSTRATED
BY KATIE LALLY

Kat vividly remembers the first time she discovered she could speak to animals. When she stood on Mr. Giggles' big bushy tail, he had cried out, "*Kaaaaat!*"

She was stunned!
Since then, she has spoken to many creatures . . .

"*Morning, Mia,*" she would cry to the friendly cow, on her way to school.
"*Hi, Freddie the frog,*" she would whisper kindly when passing by her leaping pal.

"Goodnight, Nina the owl," she would announce
to the wise bird who visits her window.

But it is only now that Kat asks herself,
"Why have I been given this gift?"

One evening after school, Kat visits her favorite person, Granny May.
She knows it will sound bizarre, but she needs to tell Granny about her gift.

In fact, to Kat's surprise, Granny confesses,
"*Well, my dear, I could once speak to our furry friends too.*"

A wave of relief washes over Kat until Granny May warns,
"*Over time, our powers weaken, my child. I wish I'd known this sooner,
but there is something you can do now!*"

*"Find Mother Nature, the earth warden who lives off Coral Cove beach.
When the tide is out, Mother Nature is about."*

"But, Granny, tell me more . . ."

"Now please hush, child. I must have my afternoon nap."

Kat leaves, feeling even more confused. But as luck would have it,
she and Mommy were heading to Coral Cove the next weekend.
She would look out for Mother Nature there.

Days feel like weeks until Kat finally arrives at Coral Cove.
Determined to find answers, she calls out with all her might,
"*Mother Nature, Mother Nature,*" not knowing what to expect.

Suddenly, in the glistening tide, a wondrous creature appears.

"Well, it's about time you got here, my dear. We have much to do!"

Mother Nature takes a deep breath and says, "Those humans are making the world very glum for our furry friends. Your Granny and I have feared about this future for decades, but we believe you can help. You were brave to come here, Kat, and even braver for talking about your power!"

"Your Granny told me how
you can talk to many animals!
I know you've been chattering to
Mia the friendly cow,

whispering with
Freddie the frog,

and even nattering with
Nina the wise owl."

"But how . . ."

"Listen up, my dear. We have much to do.
Take these seeds. They must go into the humans'
hands and deliver an important message.
They will foretell the future of our furry friends.
A very grim future. I know
the animals trust you!"

"Waaait . . ." yells Kat,
but Mother Nature slips away,
leaving Kat with a million questions
spinning around in her mind.

"Time to go, Kat,"
yells Mommy from afar.

Kat returns home with a heavy heart.
She quickly finds Mr. Giggles and tells him all about Mother Nature,
the wondrous creature with the sad eyes and the wild ideas.

"I know who can help—follow me!"

Mr. Giggles
scurries through
the field with Kat in tow.

"Look up, Kat," he begs.

"*Hello,*" hoots Nina
the wise owl.

"*I'm here,*" says
Mia the friendly cow.

"*Don't forget me,*" cries Freddie the frog.

Together they hatch a magnificent plan.
"I can tell our friends in the water to spread the seeds,"
says Freddie the frog.

"I will spread them by land,"
says Mia the friendly cow.

"*And I will spread the seeds in the sky,*"
says Nina the owl.

One by one, the rest of the animals learn that Kat—
one of the few humans on planet earth
who can talk to animals—needs their help!

By air, sea, and land, the seeds reach the hands of the humans
and begin sowing a spectacular story in their minds.

A spectacularly sad story about what life
will be like for our animal friends everywhere
if those humans don't stop hurting planet earth.

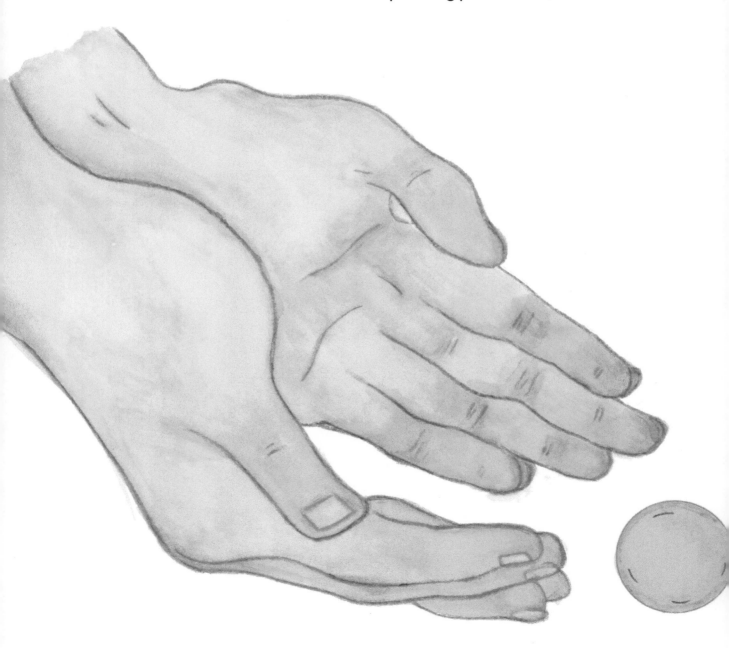

When the seeds eventually take hold, the people tremble with terror. Even the president gets one!

They see a world covered in waste with no beauty.
Rubbish fills the oceans, tall buildings steal the forests,
and even burning fuel melts the home of the polar bears!
The people know they are taking too much from the animals.

The humans cry and sob. They feel very sorry
about the spectacularly sad story from the future.

"*We must make a change!*" chant the people.

Kat is restless and struggles to sleep,
wondering if this wild and wonderful plan will really work.

Suddenly, she hears *tap tap tap* coming from her window.

"*We did it,*" announces Nina the wise owl.

"*I can't believe it,*" cries Kat, as she bounces out of bed in delight.

Word travels fast!

But amid all the joy, Kat is left with a little wobbly,
worried feeling in the pit of her belly. She knows change is no easy feat,
but if the humans work together…

They will most definitely stop the spectacularly sad story coming true!

Kat swears an almighty oath—to always be a keeper of the animal kingdom!

"I can't wait to tell Granny May the good news."

January 22'

To Lisa and Sadie

I hope you enjoy my
book.
Well Wishes
Katie.

About the Author

Katie Lally is an author and illustrator from County Mayo. When Katie is not writing and illustrating, she is a creative psychotherapist for children and teenagers in County Dublin. Katie loves the spirit and beautiful imagination of children. This continues to inspire her every day.